Cheer Up

Read more UNICORN and YETI books!

UNICORN and YETI

Cheer Up

written by
Heather Ayris Burnell

art by
Hazel Quintanilla

ACORN™
SCHOLASTIC INC.

For Noah, my BFF! — HAB

To Patricia and Hector.
You always know how to cheer me up. — HQ

Text copyright © 2020 by Heather Ayris Burnell
Illustrations copyright © 2020 by Hazel Quintanilla

Library of Congress Cataloging-in-Publication Data

Names: Burnell, Heather Ayris, author. | Quintanilla, Hazel, 1982- illustrator. |
Burnell, Heather Ayris. Unicorn and Yeti ; 4.
Title: Cheer up / by Heather Ayris Burnell; illustrated by Hazel Quintanilla.
Description: New York : Acorn/Scholastic Inc., 2020. |
Series: Unicorn and Yeti ; 4 | Summary: Unicorn and Yeti are best friends even though
they do not always like the same things—and best friends support each other and share
experiences, whether it is icicles in the snow or a walk in the dark forest.
Identifiers: LCCN 2019036270 | ISBN 9781338627695 (paperback) | ISBN 9781338627701 (library binding)
Subjects: LCSH: Unicorns—Juvenile fiction. | Yeti—Juvenile fiction. |
Best friends—Juvenile fiction. | CYAC: Unicorns—Fiction. |
Yeti—Fiction. | Best friends—Fiction. | Friendship—Fiction.
Classification: LCC PZ7.B92855 Ch 2020 | DDC [E]—dc23 LC record available at https://lccn.loc.gov/2019036270

10 9 8 7 6 5 4 3 2   20 21 22 23 24

Printed in China   62

First edition, October 2020

Edited by Katie Carella
Book design by Sarah Dvojack

Table of Contents

The Gift

Unicorn snuck up on Yeti.

Yeti, I brought you something!

4

8

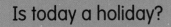

I just want to give you a gift.
That is nice.
But I do not have a gift for you.
I did not get you a gift because I wanted **you** to get **me** one.

11

I still feel bad because I do not have a gift for you.

Cheer up, Yeti. Getting a gift is supposed to be fun!

I **do** wonder what it is.

RATTLE
RATTLE

RATTLE
RATTLE

Finally, Yeti opened the gift.

You are right.
I **love** this gift!

BEST FRIENDS

14

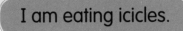

What are you eating?

I am eating icicles.

Crunch.
Crunch!
CRUNCH!

Your crunching is **very** loud.

Icicles are **very** crunchy!

Crunch.

And crunching is fun!

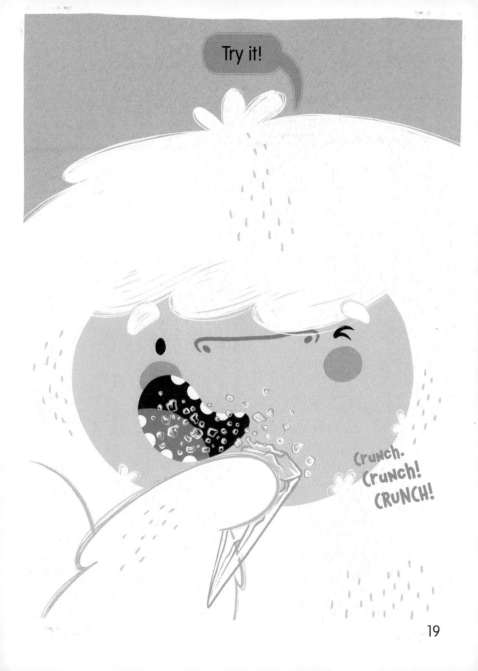

Crunch.

Crunch!

CRUNCH!

22

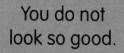
You do not look so good.

Brrr..

Crunching icicles is making me cold.

Brrr!

25

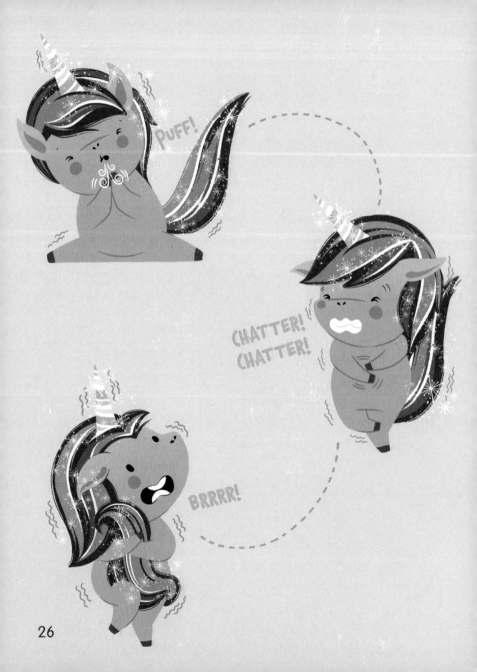

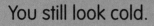

Yeti knitted a hat.

This hat will warm you up right away!

Thank you!

Yeti knitted a scarf.

Thank you.
I like this scarf.

30

Crunching icicles made you **very** cold.
Crunching icicles made me **very, very** cold!
Brrr.
Crunch.

You need mittens. Then you will be warm.

Yeti knitted mittens.

You are very good at knitting. You are fast too.

I can knit fast now.
I am getting so much
practice!

32

I know what will warm you up. A body suit!

You will not be cold at all.

I am not sure I can wear **all** of these things.

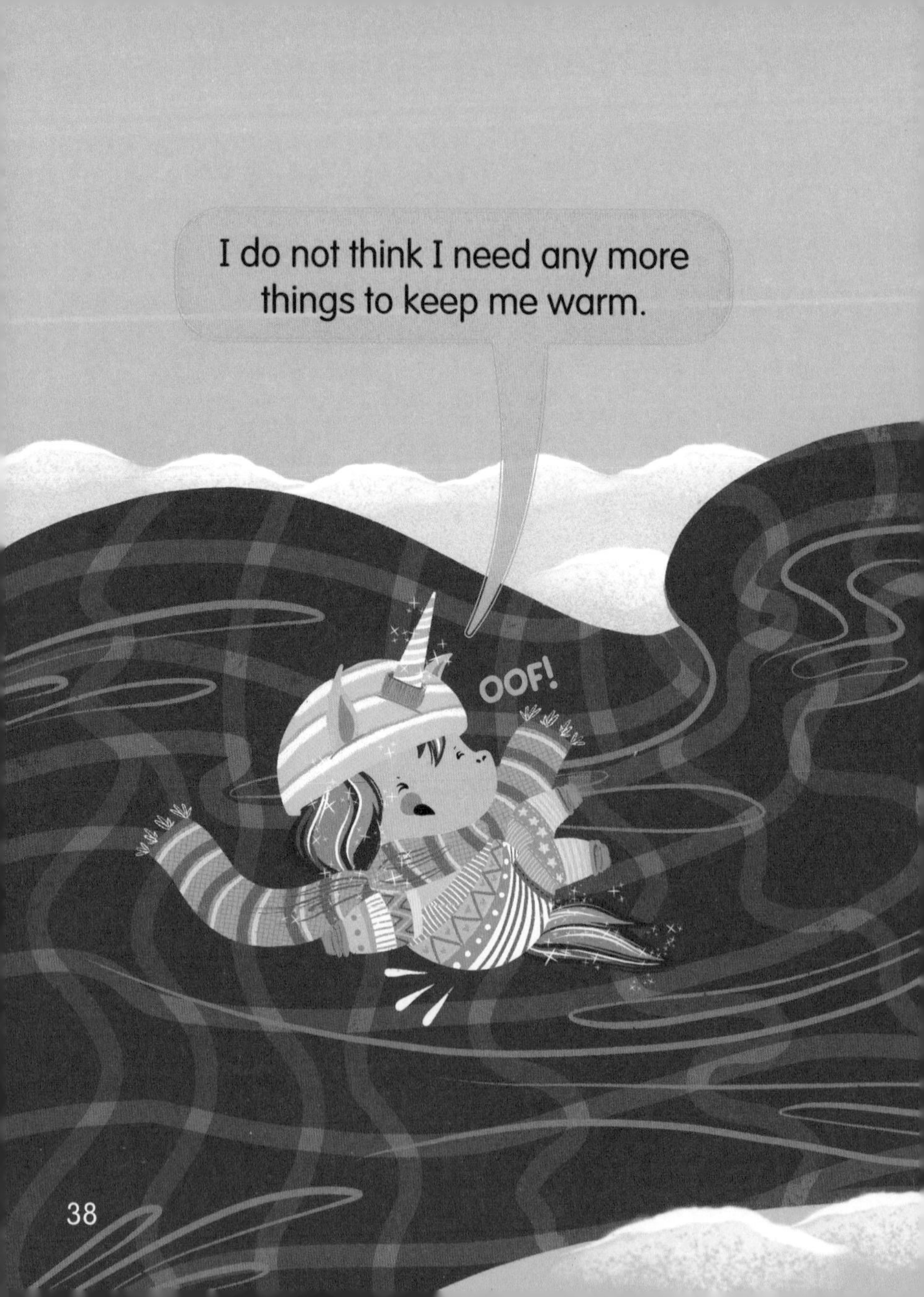
I do not think I need any more things to keep me warm.
OOF!

Don't worry.
You do not have to wear this.

Yeti knitted. And knitted. And knitted.

And a warm place to sit is
a cozy place to crunch icicles!
It is also a cozy place to drink tea!
Sip.
Sip.
Sip.
Crunch.
Crunch.
Crunch!

Let's Go!

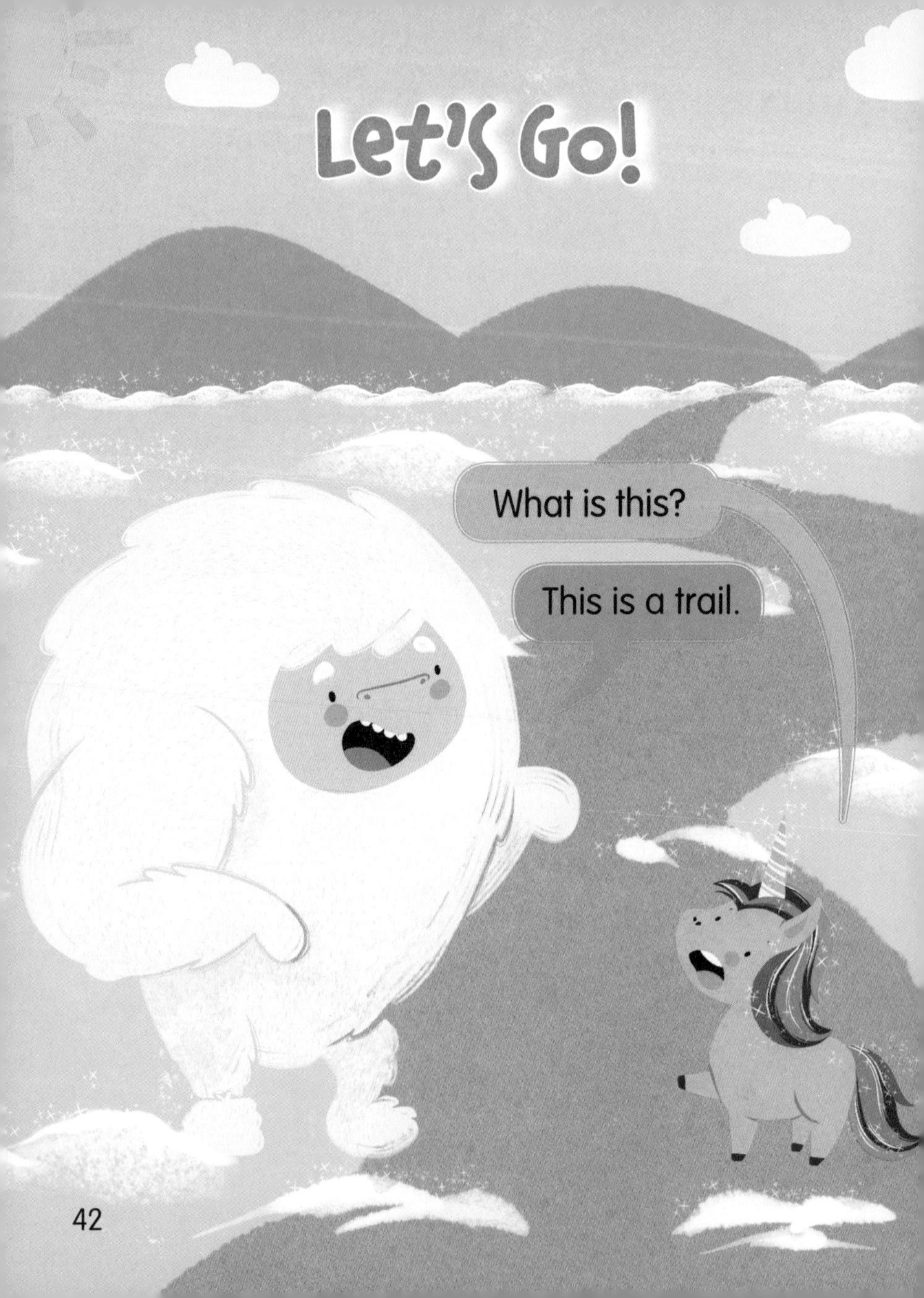

Who is the trail for?
It is for anyone who wants to go on a walk.
I would like to go on a walk.
Let's go!

Unicorn and Yeti walked up a hill.

Unicorn and Yeti walked down a hill.

I like this trail!

Are we at the end of the trail?
No. We are just getting to the best part.
Are we going in there?
Yes!

Unicorn and Yeti followed the trail into the forest.

There is not a lot of sun in here.

No. But the forest is **amazing**.

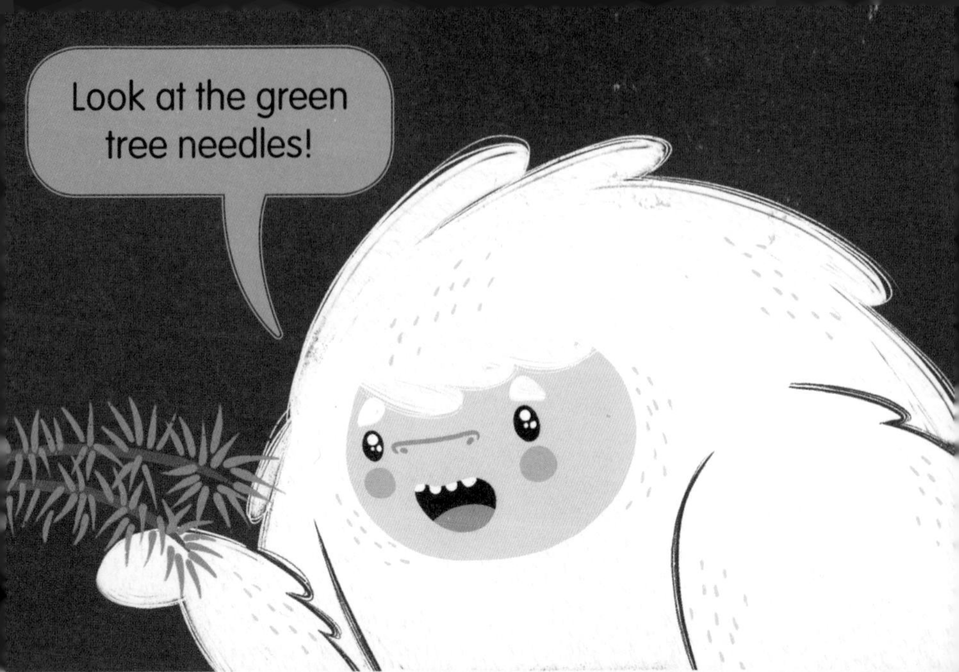
Look at the green tree needles!

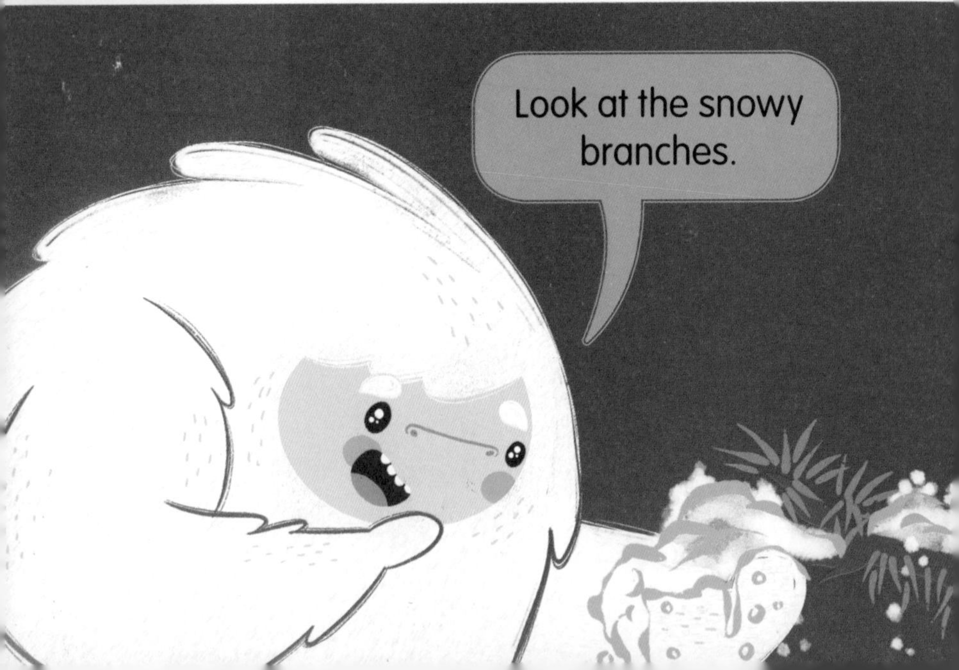
Look at the snowy branches.

49

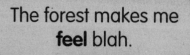

The forest makes me **feel** blah.

I am sorry that you feel blah.
But the trees and snow are **not** blah.

They are pretty!

Wow.

Now I can see the amazing green tree needles!
Now I can see the amazing snowy branches!

Yeti, you are right!
The forest **is** amazing.

About the Creators

Heather Ayris Burnell lives in Washington State where she loves taking walks on all sorts of trails. In the winter, she sometimes gets so cold that she feels like she turns blue! Luckily, she has her favorite knitted hat to help keep her warm.  Heather is a librarian and the author of the Unicorn and Yeti early reader series.

 **Hazel Quintanilla** lives in Guatemala. Hazel always knew she wanted to be an artist. When she was a kid, she carried a pencil and a notebook everywhere.

Hazel illustrates children's books, magazines, and games! And she has a secret: Unicorn and Yeti remind Hazel of her sister and brother. Her siblings are silly, funny, and quirky — just like Unicorn and Yeti!

YOU CAN DRAW YETI'S KNITTING BAG!

1 Draw the bag shape lightly with a pencil. (You will erase some of this as you go along.)

2 Add a pocket to the front of the bag. Add a bag strap. Draw a button on the strap.

3 Draw two circles that overlap each other and the top of the bag. These are yarn balls!

4 Draw three more yarn balls. Give the pocket a button with a string.

5 Draw lines on the yarn balls. And don't forget to add the knitting needles!

6 Color in your drawing!

WHAT'S YOUR STORY?

Unicorn gets very cold. Yeti helps Unicorn get warm.
Yeti knits Unicorn a hat, mittens, and more.
How would **you** help Unicorn get warm?
Write and draw your story!